Thunder-Boomer!

Thunder-Boomer!

BY Shutta Crum   ILLUSTRATED BY Carol Thompson

Clarion Books
Houghton Mifflin Harcourt
Boston • New York
2009

miaOooW!

Clarion Books
215 Park Avenue South, New York, NY 10003
Text copyright © 2009 by Shutta Crum
Illustrations copyright © 2009 by Carol Thompson

Hand lettering by John Stevens.
The illustrations were executed in watercolor, gouache, pastel, crayon, and collage.
The text was set in 13.5-point Clearface Gothic.

For information about permission to reproduce selections from this book, write to
Permissions, Houghton Mifflin Harcourt Publishing Company, 215 Park Avenue South, New York, NY 10003.

Clarion Books is an imprint of Houghton Mifflin Harcourt Publishing Company.

www.clarionbooks.com

Printed in Singapore

Library of Congress Cataloging-in-Publication Data

Crum, Shutta
Thunder-Boomer! / by Shutta Crum ; illustrated by Carol Thompson.
p. cm.
Summary: A farm family scurries for shelter from a violent thunderstorm that
brings welcome relief from the heat and also an unexpected surprise.
ISBN: 978-0-618-61865-1
[1. Thunderstorms—Fiction. 2. Farm life—Fiction.] I. Thompson, Carol, ill. II. Title
PZ7.C888288 Th 2009
[E]—22

2008010478

TWP   10 9 8 7 6 5 4 3 2

For Abigail, my wonderful whirlwind of a granddaughter, with love
—S. C.

For Andrea B.
—C. T.

The day is hot.

Dad plows, his tractor glinting in the sun.

Tom slaps his feet against the surface of the pond.

I sprawl in the shade of the chestnut tree.

Scooter pants with his tongue hanging out.

Mother comes down the path to settle on the dock.

"I hope this heat breaks soon," she says.

"We need a thunder-boomer."

7

Suddenly, there's a soft-touch tease.

A leaf tips over . . . and then another.

"Mmm. Feel that breeze," says Tom.

Scrambling to my feet, I stretch my arms

and try to catch each welcome gust of wind.

But then the air turns chilly. Dark clouds hide the sun.

The wind stirs up the pond and rustles through the corn.

Mother looks around and says, "It's time to head on back.

A storm is on the way."

"Ahhhh!"

8

9

We scurry home across the fields.

Dad drives the tractor in and slides the barn door shut.

Tom runs and flaps his arms to coop the squawking chickens,

while Mother and I race to yank the laundry from the line.

Scooter follows. He wants to play.

Jumping high, he snatches something white.

"Stop that, Scooter. Drop it!" I yell, and for once he listens.

Then suddenly: a lightning flash—and the wind steals away his prize.

"Let it go!" Mother shouts and grabs the laundry basket.

ZZZZt!

"Oops!"

Thunder rumbles all around. We run up on the porch,

and Tom and Scooter join us. The last one in is Dad.

He bounds across the yard just as the clouds crack open.

Then, as if someone's turned a faucet on,

the rain comes gushing down . . .

and down . . .

and down.

Rumble-brum-brum.

Splash! Sploosh!

Something flutters by the shed. I squint into the rain.

It's Maizey, my favorite chicken! She's caught out in the storm.

Dad sighs and jams his hat on tight.

He dashes into the downpour, jumping over puddles.

Scooter barks and tags along. They're off to rescue Maizey.

Dad bends to scoop her up. She balks—and pecks him!

What's wrong? That's not like her at all.

Bawk!
Squawk!

As soon as they return,

Mother herds us all inside.

Dad is drenched, from draggled hat to soggy shoes.

He slips and squishes by, carrying grumpy Maizey.

Scooter's claws *click-clack* until he gets his footing.

Then starting from his drippy head, he twists and shakes—

and splatters us with rain!

Dad puts Maizey down, and she stalks across the floor,

complaining with each haughty step.

Mother sops up puddles,

while Tom and I rush room to room, slamming windows shut.

Boom! Boom!

Zzzzt!

Zzzzt Cr-a-a-ck!

Rumble-brum-brum-brum...brum...brum

18

Zzzzt! Rumble . . . .

Swish-wack!
Thump-WUMP!

There's another bolt of lightning, and when the thunder follows,
it makes the whole house shake.
Scooter's scared! He hides his head beneath the couch,
but the rest of him won't fit.
A thunder-boomer's here!

Gusting rain pelts the roof.
The maple's branches brush and *wump* against the walls.
Then something white goes whipping past the window—
through the air.

"Dad's underwear!"

19

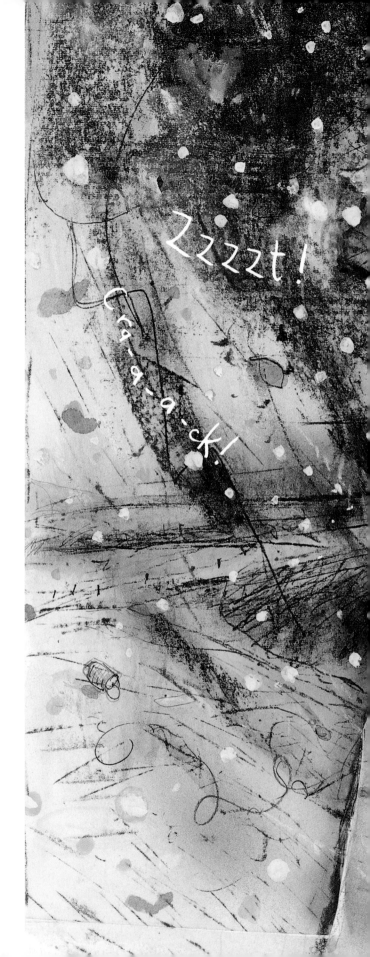

Tom and I start laughing, and when we finally stop,

we hear a pinging sound.

"Oh, no," Dad mutters. "Hail." And he slumps into his chair.

Hail could shred the corn's green leaves.

It could dent our metal roofs.

Scooter whines—he doesn't like the noise.

I put my arms around him and stroke his quivering side.

"Shhh, it's all right," I tell him.

"That's just the thunder-boomer showing off."

Then the hail comes clinking down, ringing harder, louder, faster!

Just when I think it will never end, there's a sudden—*hush*.

No one speaks.

The wind has stopped, and the branches of the maple

have finally settled down.

The only thing I hear . . . is a single, little sound.

ping!

Scooter pulls his head out.

"See? It's over, boy," I say. "That mean old storm is gone."

Suddenly, Maizey flutters from Dad's chair,

where she's been sulking for a while.

She marches through the kitchen, straight up to the door.

Scooter scrambles after her. They both want out right now!

22

We go outside to a world that's wet and deeply green.

The puddles in the yard are full of floating hail and leaves.

Our metal roofs are dimpled—just a bit.

And the corn is leaning—but not ruined.

Scooter sniffs and noses around, his tail high in the air.

He hauls up something soggy and drags it through the mud.

It's Dad's underwear!

"yuck!"

"give it here!"

25

"Hey! Come back!"

Dad chases after Scooter.

Tom and Mom join in.

But I am watching Maizey as she clucks around the shed.

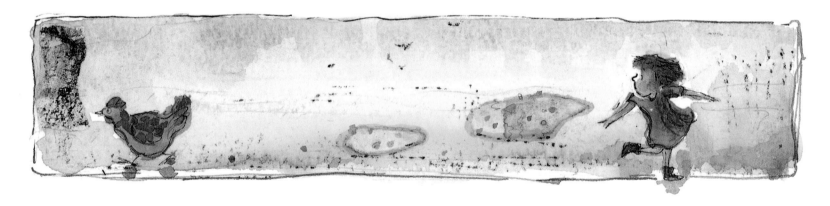

She peeks and pokes and bobs her head.

What is she searching for? Why has she been so grouchy?

Suddenly, she ruffs her feathers.

What has she found?

27

Maizey shelters something small—something wet.

I reach beneath her wing . . .

"Look!"

Purr-um-brum-brum. . .
Purr-um-brum. . .

It's a kitten—all soaked and shivery from the storm.

I hold him close. I stroke his rain-slicked fur.

He licks my thumb and . . . rumbles!

Purr-um-brum
brum...Purr-um-
brum

29

"Well," Dad says. "The storm has left a gift."

"May we keep him? Please?" I ask. "We could name him Stormy."

"No," says Tom. "He should be Thor—the mighty god of Thunder!"

Mother says, "He *needs* a name." She looks Dad in the eye.

Dad shakes his head and sighs. "Ooo-kay. We'll keep this gift.

Just listen to that thunderous purr!"

And then I say, "I know the perfect name!

Let's call him Thunder-Boomer."

31

Now the air smells sweet as butter . . .

everything's washed clean.

The puddles have dried up.

The clouds have traveled on.

And all I hear are quiet evening sounds—

the call of owls beyond the pond,

    the chuff of toads in Mother's garden,

        and the low and sleepy rumble of a tired Thunder-Boomer.

oooooöh-wo-woö o

chuuur-uh, chuh

Purr-um-brum-brum...rum...